A SONG OF SUN and SKY

To every artist who has had to fight, and continues
to fight, to find their place in the world —J. C.

Henry Holt and Company, *Publishers since 1866* • Henry Holt® is a registered trademark of Macmillan Publishing
Group, LLC • 120 Broadway, New York, NY 10271 • mackids.com

Copyright © 2023 by Jason Cockcroft. All rights reserved.

Our books may be purchased in bulk for promotional, educational, or business use. Please contact your local
bookseller or the Macmillan Corporate and Premium Sales Department at (800) 221-7945 ext. 5442 or by email at
MacmillanSpecialMarkets@macmillan.com.

Library of Congress Cataloging-in-Publication Data is available.

First edition, 2023 • Book design by Mercedes Pardo • Created with digital art with scanned pencil work and watercolor
washes • Printed in China by Hung Hing Off-set Printing Co. Ltd., Heshan City, Guangdong Province

ISBN 978-1-250-81943-7 (hardcover)
1 3 5 7 9 10 8 6 4 2

A SONG OF SUN AND SKY

Jason Cockcroft

GODWINBOOKS

Henry Holt and Company

New York

The first color was orange.

Everywhere she looked was orange.
The ground and the sky and the dust on the window.
Orange.

The second color was gray.
Every time it appeared, her father's face would grow hot
and red, which was the third color. The one Lula didn't like.

"Let's see if we can get some water from the house over here," he said, taking her hand and leading her across the dry, empty earth of stone, cacti, and bright dirt.

The fourth color she saw was white.
It was the color of the skulls on the wall.

And it was the color of the old lady's hair.
And of the milk she poured for Lula while her father
and the lady talked.

When the lady and her father were done, he told her they'd be around for a while, so she might as well explore. But not too far.

She wandered into the gardens.
She looked at the stones and at
the little cacti in the dirt.
And at the lizards.

Lula liked the city, because there were yellow cabs and red roofs and green trees in the city, and people dressed in pinks and blues and purples.

But the desert just looked orange. All of it. The only real colors here were on the lady's apron.

"What are you doing?" asked Lula.

The lady had pretended she hadn't seen her. But she had.

"I'm painting," the lady said.

"But why do you use so many colors? The desert is just orange," Lula replied.

The lady didn't say she was wrong. She just kept on painting.
"What color do you think the sky is?" she asked.

That was easy. It was blue.

"And a dog?"

That was harder.

A dog could be black or yellow or gray. Or brown.
"What about red? Have you ever seen a red dog?
What color is a brown dog at sunset?" the woman asked.
Lula had to think about that.

The hills are brown and purple and yellow and red.
The plants are green, but when the sun fades and
the moon rises, they turn blue.

"Nothing's ever only one color," the lady said.

"Like at home," Lula said. "When we spray the
hose on the yard, the sun shines through the water
and there are lots of colors. Like a rainbow."

"Look at that tree," the lady said. "Right now, it's brown with bits of green, but at night it turns black. Sometimes it looks red. Sometimes stars get stuck in its branches."

"What color is sleep?" Lula asked.

"When I close my eyes in bed, there's the color of night,
all blues and purples that slip me into sleep,
like slipping slowly into a swimming pool
or swimming in the sea."

The lady said, "I haven't been swimming for a long time."

"You should," Lula told her.
"There are lots of colors in the ocean."

"The color of my anger is red," the lady said. "Like fire."

The girl nodded. She'd heard of people seeing red when they were angry.

And her father said sometimes he felt blue. Sometimes Lula felt blue, too.

"Why are you angry?" she asked.

"When I can't get a painting right, that makes me angry."

"People make me angry," Lula said. "Sometimes,
when people are mean, they reveal their true colors."

"Color is in the land. There are the colors of every bird that flew through here. There are the colors of every family, every man and woman and child. And there are the colors of all the bones buried under the soil."

"Every animal that sleeps under the stars leaves its colors behind.
At night, they all mix together and dance under the moonlight."

"They come out and play, and after a while you can't tell red from blue or green from black. It runs like ink, all together."

"Dreams have colors," Lula said. "Only when you wake up, you don't always remember them. And in the morning, it's as though nothing had ever happened. And the blue is back in the sky, and the dirt stays orange."

"And the dog standing out there is all dog-colored again, and everything is like it was in the daylight," Lula said.

The lady smiled at her. "But we know different."

Lula looked at the lady and the desert
and the dog one last time.
None of them looked the same as before.
Even her father looked different.

There was green on his skin, and blue in
his eyes, and orange all over his clothes.
There was orange on Lula, too.

"These colors will stay with you," the lady said.
"And you'll leave your colors here, too. And the color
of your bright green car when you go. And your
brown hair. And your red shirt.
    "And you'll take the colors you've found here with
you wherever you are."

"And nothing will ever be lost."

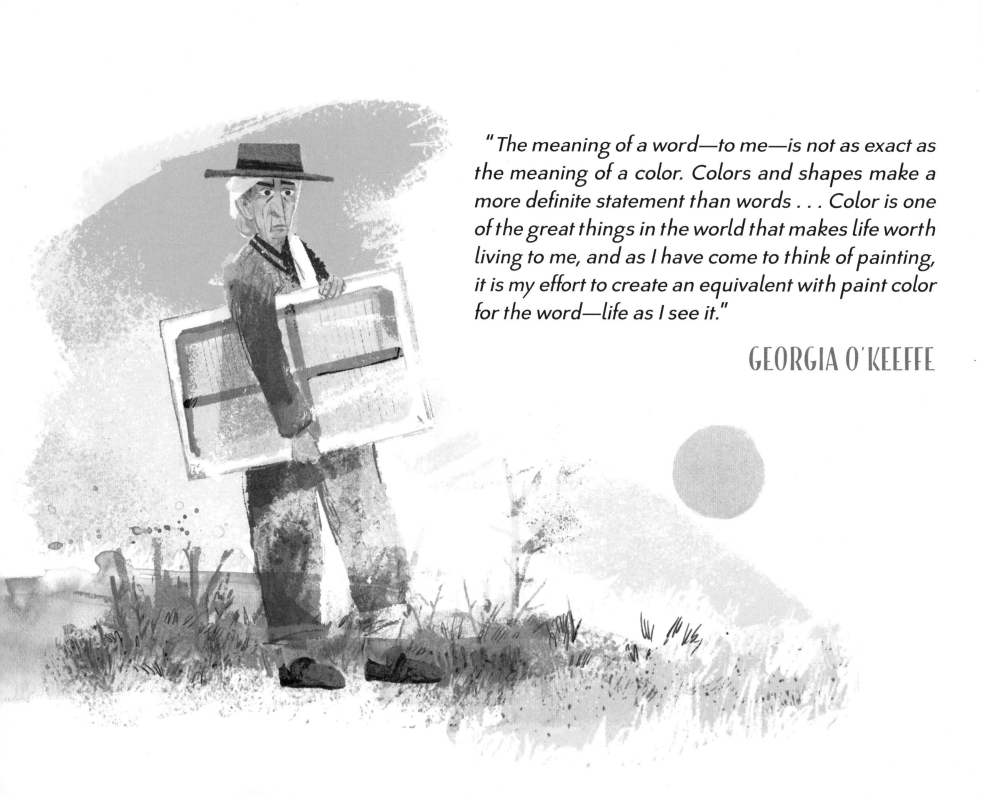

"The meaning of a word—to me—is not as exact as the meaning of a color. Colors and shapes make a more definite statement than words . . . Color is one of the great things in the world that makes life worth living to me, and as I have come to think of painting, it is my effort to create an equivalent with paint color for the word—life as I see it."

GEORGIA O'KEEFFE

GEORGIA O'KEEFFE

The artist with an eye as straight as an arrow

Georgia O'Keeffe was twelve years old when she decided to be an artist. "I had a sense of power. I always had it," she said, reflecting on her childhood. Adding, "From the time I was small . . . I was always doing things other people don't do." Even as a child, she had such a formidably unique personality that her two brothers and four sisters saw her instinctively as their leader and queen. "She had everything about her way, and if she didn't she'd raise the devil," her sister Catherine said.

Born in 1887, O'Keeffe grew up on her family's Wisconsin farm, where she learned from her mother the value of education and music and art, and from her father the idea of adventure. "I think that deep down I am like my father," she said. "When he wanted to see the country, he just got up and went." She didn't like school, but when she left, she enjoyed art lessons with a local painter. It was the same year she told a school friend she would be an artist: "I don't really know where I got my artist idea . . . I only know that by that time it was definitely settled in my mind." Later, she studied in Virginia, then at the Art Institute of Chicago and in New York, and traveled widely. Friends, fellow students,

and the pupils she taught remembered her for her unconventional character, her talent, and the way she stood out, including her appearance—she often wore black clothes, men's jackets, simple with straight lines and no frills or decorations, some of which she made herself. When she was teaching she'd break the usual pupil-student practice and take her students out hiking in the prairies or share lunch with them—and, once, she caused a minor sensation at her college by sitting barefoot with them, which was seen back then as scandalous. "There was something insatiable about her, as direct as an arrow, and completely independent," her friend Anita Pollitzer wrote.

O'Keeffe was one of the first American women artists to exhibit a purely abstract artwork. Despite how strong and confident she often seemed, early on in her career she was insecure about her talent, and she claimed to suffer all through her life from fear. "I'm frightened all the time," she once said. "Scared to death. But I've never let it stop me. Never!" Her first exhibition in New York was put on without her knowledge by the famous photographer and gallery owner Alfred Stieglitz. Incensed that he would show her drawings without her permission, she went to his gallery to remonstrate with him—a combustible meeting that would prove to be the start of a long relationship that significantly influenced both their careers. Although she claimed not to enjoy going to exhibitions, O'Keeffe had a deep understanding of art history. She never compared herself to other artists or sought inspiration from them, but she enjoyed the works of Rodin, Pissarro, Goya, and van Gogh. She was particularly drawn to Chinese art, which she acknowledged had influenced her unusual use of scale in her paintings where she transformed small, natural objects into magnified abstract shapes.

In later life she moved to New Mexico and a place called Ghost Ranch. She was drawn there by the extraordinary colors of the hills, which due to the unique local geology can appear purple and gray and red and green and yellow. There she produced some of the most widely celebrated paintings of her career. She would become a leading figure in a new art movement that challenged the tradition of figurative painting to produce work that combined elements of abstract and representational art. Her fame was due largely to a number of paintings she made that depicted botanical subjects, painted in sensual colors and usually cropped to give an effect of abstraction. At her studio in New Mexico, she treated traditionally minor still life subjects such as flowers or animal skulls with the same grandeur and scale she used to represent her landscapes. "When you take a flower in your hand and really look at it," she said, "it's your world for the moment. I wanted to give that world to someone else." Nature was a huge influence on her work, but her time in New York, too, had an impact. She'd proven she could paint not only nature, but skyscrapers and cityscapes. "When I wanted to paint New York, the men thought I'd lost my mind," she said. She wanted to give the things found in nature—flowers, stones, feathers, shells, weeds—the monumental energy and size of the city, and to slow down the viewers' attention in order for them to absorb

the beauty in their environment. "The flower . . . was so small you really could not appreciate it for itself . . . If I could paint that flower in a huge scale, then you could not ignore its beauty."

Although she was known as the Mother of American Modernism, O'Keeffe rejected the idea of belonging to any group or organization, and she valued the independence she'd struggled for throughout her life, both as a woman and an artist. By the time of her death at the age of ninety-eight, she had become by some margin the most famous woman painter of her generation.

"I grew up pretty much how everybody else grows up and one day seven years ago found myself saying to myself—I can't go where I want to—I can't do what I want to—I can't even say what I want to. School and things that painters have taught me even keep me from painting as I want to. I decided I was a very stupid fool not at least to paint as I wanted to and say what I wanted to when I painted, as that seemed to be the only thing I could do that didn't concern anybody but myself—that was nobody's business but my own."

From the start of her career, O'Keeffe had to ward off the accusations that she was a female painter with a peculiar female outlook, one that was emotional and esoteric and driven by nature. Her paintings were radical, bold, and groundbreaking, and she was determined for them to be viewed with the same critical eye as the work of any male painter. She didn't hide her irritation at the narrow way critics—both men and women—defined her. That same determination had been evident in her as a child, and it stayed with her throughout her long life. She was still painting watercolors at the age of eighty-nine.

When she was asked how she would like to be remembered, she answered, "As a painter—just as a painter."

Acknowledgments

The books below were an invaluable source of information and inspiration:

Georgia O'Keeffe: A Life by Roxana Robinson (HarperCollins, 1989)

Georgia O'Keeffe: American And Modern by Charles C. Eldredge (Yale and University Press, 1996)

Georgia O'Keeffe at Home by Alicai Inez Guzmán (Frances Lincoln, 2017)

Georgia O'Keeffe and Her Houses by Barbara Buhler Lynes and Agapita Lopez (Harry N. Abrams, 2012)